For my teachers Juan Luis Morales Rojas,
Elizabeth Azócar, Ricardo Ferrada, and Soledad Bianchi

More praise for Alejandro Zambra:

'When I read Zambra I feel like someone's shooting fireworks inside my head. His prose is as compact as a grain of gunpowder, but its allusions and ramifications branch out and illuminate even the most remote corners of our minds' Valeria Luiselli, author of *The Story of My Teeth*

'*Multiple Choice* is unlike anything I've ever encountered before . . . a wonderfully disconcerting and unforgettable experience' Francisco Goldman, author of *Say Her Name*

'There is no writer like Alejandro Zambra, no one as bold, as subtle, as funny. *Multiple Choice* is his most accomplished work yet . . . This book is not to be missed' Daniel Alarcón, author of *At Night We Walk in Circles*

'Falling in love with Zambra's literature is a fascinating road to travel. Imaginative and original, he is a master of short forms; I adore his devastating audacity' Enrique Vila-Matas, author of *The Illogic of Kassel*

'Zambra's field of enquiry overspills the historical and political. It spreads far beyond Chilean borders and slips the bounds of narrative to question the very idea of a single, correct and definitive answer' *Sunday Herald*

A7 034 017 X

ALSO BY ALEJANDRO ZAMBRA

Bonsai
The Private Lives of Trees
Ways of Going Home
My Documents

ALEJANDRO ZAMBRA

MULTIPLE CHOICE

TRANSLATED FROM THE SPANISH BY
MEGAN McDOWELL

GRANTA

Granta Publications, 12 Addison Avenue, London W11 4QR

First published in Great Britain by Granta Books in 2016
This paperback edition published by Granta Books in 2017

First published the USA in 2016 by Penguin Books, an imprint of Penguin Random
House LLC, New York

Originally published in Spanish as *Facsimil* by Editorial Huerders, Santiago de Chile.

A selection from this book appeared in *The New Yorker* under the title
'Reading Comprehension: Test No. 1'

A CIP catalogue record for this book is available from the British Library.

13 5 7 9 10 8 6 4 2

ISBN 978 1 78378 271 0 (paperback)
ISBN 978 1 78378 270 3 (ebook)

Set in Adobe Caslon Pro with Knockout Display
Designed by Elke Sigal
Offset by Avon DataSet Ltd, Bidford on Avon, B50 4JH

Printed and bound by CPI Group (UK) Ltd, Croydon, CR0 4YY

www.grantabooks.com

CONTENTS

I. EXCLUDED TERM

In exercises 1 through 24, mark the answer that corresponds to the word whose meaning has no relation to either the heading or the other words listed.

1. **MULTIPLE**

   A) manifold
   B) numerous
   C) untold
   D) five
   E) two

2. **CHOICE**

   A) voice
   B) one
   C) decision
   D) preference
   E) alternative

3. **YOURS**

   A) hers
   B) his
   C) mine
   D) their
   E) ours

4. **FIVE**

   A) six
   B) seven
   C) eight
   D) nine
   E) one

5. **BLINK**

   A) sweat
   B) nod
   C) cough
   D) cry
   E) bite

6. **BODY**

   A) dust
   B) ashes
   C) dirt
   D) grit
   E) smut

7. **Mask**

   A) disguise
   B) veil
   C) hood
   D) face
   E) confront

8. **Bear**

   A) endure
   B) tolerate
   C) abide
   D) panda
   E) kangaroo

9. **Teach**

   A) preach
   B) control
   C) educate
   D) initiate
   E) screech

10. COPY

   A) cut
   B) paste
   C) cut
   D) paste
   E) undo

11. LETTER

   A) uppercase
   B) lowercase
   C) cursive
   D) dead
   E) silent

12. CUT

   A) erase
   B) annul
   C) blot
   D) expunge
   E) wound

13. HEARTBREAKING

A) breathtaking
B) earthshaking
C) lovemaking
D) forsaking
E) mistaking

14. BLACKLIST

A) backlist
B) checklist
C) playlist
D) shitlist
E) novelist

15. CHILDHOOD

A) childlike
B) childproof
C) childcare
D) childless
E) childfree

16. **PROTECT**

A) care for

B) cover for

C) dote on

D) watch over

E) look after

17. **PROMISE**

A) complete

B) silence

C) promise

D) complete

E) silence

18. **PRAY**

A) please

B) praise

C) prey

D) prays

E) pleas

19. **BLACKOUT**

   A) whiteout
   B) pitch-black
   C) lights-out
   D) nightfall
   E) dead of night

20. **RAZE**

   A) flatten
   B) raise
   C) level
   D) demolish
   E) subdue

21. **SPARE**

   A) time
   B) room
   C) change
   D) tire
   E) life

22. **PAUSE**

    A) hesitation
    B) recess
    C) break
    D) breath
    E) silence

23. **SILENCE**

    A) fidelity
    B) complicity
    C) loyalty
    D) conspiracy
    E) cowardice

24. **SILENCE**

    A) silence
    B) silence
    C) silence
    D) silence
    E) silence

II. SENTENCE ORDER

In exercises 25 through 36, mark the answer that puts the sentences in the best possible order to form a coherent text.

25. Nineteen eighty-something

1. Your father argued with your mother.
2. Your mother argued with your brother.
3. Your brother argued with your father.
4. It was almost always cold.
5. That is all you remember.

A) 2 – 3 – 1 – 4 – 5
B) 3 – 1 – 2 – 4 – 5
C) 4 – 1 – 2 – 3 – 5
D) 4 – 5 – 1 – 2 – 3
E) 5 – 1 – 2 – 3 – 4

26. The second

1. You try to remember your first Communion.
2. You try to remember your first masturbation.
3. You try to remember the first time you had sex.
4. You try to remember the first death in your life.
5. And the second.

A) 1 – 5 – 2 – 3 – 4
B) 1 – 2 – 5 – 3 – 4
C) 1 – 2 – 3 – 5 – 4
D) 4 – 5 – 1 – 2 – 3
E) 4 – 3 – 2 – 1 – 5

27. A child

1. You dream that you lose a child.
2. You wake up.
3. You cry.
4. You lose a child.
5. You cry.

A) 1 – 2 – 4 – 3 – 5
B) 1 – 2 – 3 – 5 – 4
C) 2 – 3 – 4 – 5 – 1
D) 3 – 4 – 5 – 1 – 2
E) 4 – 5 – 3 – 1 – 2

28. Your house

1.   It belongs to a bank, but you prefer to think of it
     as yours.
2.   If all goes well, you'll finish paying for it in 2033.
3.   You've lived here for eleven years. First with a family,
     and later on with some ghosts who ended up leaving, too.
4.   You don't like the neighborhood. There are no parks
     nearby and the air is dirty.
5.   But you love this house. You'll never leave it.

A)   2 – 3 – 4 – 5 – 1
B)   3 – 4 – 5 – 1 – 2
C)   4 – 5 – 1 – 2 – 3
D)   3 – 1 – 2 – 4 – 5
E)   1 – 2 – 4 – 3 – 5

29. **Birthday**

1. You wake up early, go for a walk, look for a café.
2. It's your birthday, but you don't remember.
3. You feel like you are forgetting something, but it's only a sense of unease, an intuition that something is out of place.
4. You go about your routine, like any other Saturday.
5. You smoke, turn on the TV, fall asleep listening to the midnight news.

A) 5 – 1 – 2 – 3 – 4
B) 4 – 5 – 1 – 2 – 3
C) 3 – 4 – 5 – 1 – 2
D) 2 – 3 – 4 – 5 – 1
E) 1 – 2 – 3 – 4 – 5

30. Two hundred twenty-three

1.   You remember the freckles on her breasts, on her legs, on her belly, on her ass. The exact number: two hundred twenty-three. One thousand two hundred and seven days ago there were two hundred twenty-three.

2.   You reread the messages she used to send you: They are beautiful, funny. Long paragraphs, vivid, complex sentences. Warm words. She writes better than you do.

3.   You remember the time you drove five hours just to see her for ten minutes. It wasn't ten minutes, it was the whole afternoon, but you like to think it was only ten minutes.

4.   You remember the waves, the rocks. Her sandals, a wound on her foot. You remember your eyes darting from her thighs to her eyelashes.

5.   You never got used to being with her. You never got used to being without her. You remember when she said, in a whisper, as if to herself: *Everything is OK.*

A)   5 – 1 – 2 – 3 – 4
B)   4 – 5 – 1 – 2 – 3
C)   3 – 4 – 5 – 1 – 2
D)   2 – 3 – 4 – 5 – 1
E)   1 – 2 – 3 – 4 – 5

31. Relatives

1. You group them into two lists: the ones you love and the ones you don't.
2. You group them into two lists: the ones who shouldn't be alive and the ones who shouldn't be dead.
3. You group them according to the degree of trust they inspired in you as a child.
4. For a moment you think you discover something important, something that has been weighing on you for years.
5. You group them into two lists: the living and the dead.

A) 1 – 3 – 4 – 5 – 2
B) 5 – 2 – 1 – 3 – 4
C) 1 – 3 – 5 – 2 – 4
D) 3 – 4 – 5 – 2 – 1
E) 1 – 2 – 3 – 4 – 5

32. A kick in the balls

1. You think of all the people, living or dead, near or far, men or women, from your country or abroad, who have reason to kick you in the balls.
2. You wonder if you deserve a kick in the balls.
3. You wonder if you deserve to be hated. You wonder if anyone really hates you.
4. You wonder if you hate anyone. You wonder if you hate the people who hate you.
5. Insomnia wounds and accompanies you.

A)   1 – 1 – 1 – 1 – 1
B)   2 – 2 – 2 – 2 – 2
C)   3 – 3 – 3 – 3 – 3
D)   4 – 4 – 4 – 4 – 4
E)   5 – 5 – 5 – 5 – 5

33. Rhyme

1. You search for words that rhyme with your first name.
2. You search for words that rhyme with your last name.
3. Your first and last names do not rhyme, but you search for words that rhyme with both your first and last names.
4. You search for words that don't rhyme with either your first name or your last name, or with anything else.
5. You are not crazy.

A) 5 – 1 – 2 – 3 – 4
B) 5 – 4 – 3 – 2 – 1
C) 1 – 2 – 3 – 4 – 5
D) 1 – 5 – 2 – 3 – 4
E) 1 – 2 – 3 – 4

34. First person

1. You believe the only solution is to keep your mouth shut.
2. You never say *I*.
3. Thanks to several bottles of wine, you learn to say *I*.
4. You never say *we*.
5. Thanks to a bottle of pisco, you learn to say *we*.
6. You are rehabilitated.

A) 1 – 2 – 3 – 4 – 5 – 6
B) 1 – 2 – 4 – 3 – 5 – 6
C) 2 – 4 – 1 – 3 – 5 – 6
D) 4 – 5 – 6 – 2 – 3 – 1
E) 2 – 3 – 6 – 4 – 5 – 1

35. Swimming

1. The scale says 92.1 kilos. You tune the radio to 92.1 FM. You loathe this station, every program on it. You have to lose weight.

2. You're at the public pool. Sitting on the edge with your feet in the water, you watch some kids who are learning how to swim. The teacher is emphatic, her voice does not sound sweet. The children look very serious.

3. When you were a kid, you were in love with silence. Later, you wanted words to flood you, sink you. But you already knew how to swim, no one had to teach you. They just threw us into the water, you think, and like dogs, we learned to swim right away.

4. Or maybe they taught you in school. Maybe that was the only thing they taught you. Not to swim, but to move your arms and legs. And to hold your breath for hours.

5. Everyone knows that swimming is the best exercise. You're going to be OK, you think to yourself, you're going to lose weight. You dive into the cold water. Swimming strengthens your muscles and your memory.

A) 1 – 2 – 3 – 4 – 5
B) 1 – 2 – 3 – 4 – 5
C) 1 – 2 – 3 – 4 – 5
D) 1 – 2 – 3 – 4 – 5
E) 1 – 2 – 3 – 4 – 5

36. Scars

1. You think about how the shortest distance between two points is the length of a scar.
2. You think: the introduction is the father, the climax is the son, and the resolution is the holy spirit.
3. You read books that are much stranger than the books you would write if you wrote.
4. You think, as if it were a discovery, that the last point in the line of time is the present.
5. You try to go from the general to the specific, even if the general is General Pinochet.
6. You try to go from the abstract to the concrete.
7. The abstract is the pain of others.
8. The concrete is the pain of others colliding with your body until you are completely invaded.
9. The concrete is something that can only grow.
10. Something like a tumor, or the opposite of a tumor: a child.
11. In your case, it's a tumor.

A) 1 – 2 – 3 – 4 – 5 – 6 – 7 – 8 – 9 – 10 – 11
B) 1 – 2 – 3 – 4 – 5 – 6 – 7 – 8 – 9 – 10 – 11
C) 1 – 2 – 3 – 4 – 5 – 6 – 7 – 8 – 9 – 10 – 11
D) 1 – 2 – 3 – 4 – 5 – 6 – 7 – 8 – 9 – 10 – 11
E) 1 – 2 – 3 – 4 – 5 – 6 – 7 – 8 – 9 – 10 – 11

III. SENTENCE COMPLETION

In exercises 37 through 54, complete the sentence using the appropriate elements. Mark the answer that best fits the sentence.

37. _____ the thousand amendments they've made to it, the Chilean Constitution of 1980 is a piece of shit.

    A)   After
    B)   Due to
    C)   In spite of
    D)   Thanks to
    E)   Notwithstanding

38. I often used to lie, _____ I wore dark glasses.

    A)   but
    B)   though
    C)   so
    D)   but even so,
    E)   but only when

39. A lot of people want me dead, _____ I'm not _____ ill.

    A)   but   that
    B)   though   actually
    C)   even though   gravely
    D)   yet   even
    E)   though   yet

40. Students go to university to _____ , not to _____ .

A) study   think
B) study   protest
C) drink   think
D) sleep   die
E) buy   window-shop

41. And if they have any _____ left, that's what _____ for.

A) energy   sports are
B) hope   reality is
C) illusions   the void is
D) dissent   the cops are
E) neurons   crack cocaine is

42. What is impossible for _____ is possible for _____ .

A) men   God
B) men   women
C) the right   the left
D) Rebecca   Becky
E) the poor   the rich

43. What is impossible for _____ is possible for _____ .

A) my mom   my dad
B) Pisces   Leo
C) me   you
D) McCartney   Lennon
E) tomorrow   the day after tomorrow

44. If the _____ within you grows _____ , how deep is your _____ !

A) light   dark   darkness
B) confusion   light   flashlight
C) candor   lustful   schlong
D) love   furious   divorce
E) humor   bitter   book

45. If someone strikes you on the right _____ , offer him the other as well.

A) cheek
B) week
C) wing
D) chord
E) time

46. I want to gather these words together, _____ nothing makes any sense.

A) though
B) so that
C) even if
D) but
E) until

47. I seek words that _____ appear in books.

A) sometimes
B) never
C) always
D) only
E) don't even

48. You are not _____, you are not _____, you are not _____.

A)	good	bad	wrong
B)	wrong	right	here
C)	here	there	gone
D)	gone	around	mine
E)	mine	mine	mine

49. Last night I dreamed you were _____ and I was _____ and we were _____ together.

A)	here	here	lying
B)	coming	coming	coming
C)	lost	lost	walking
D)	lost	not	not
E)	sick	dead	almost

50. Last night I dreamed you were a _____ and I was a _____ and we were _____ together.

A)	dog	dog	barking
B)	leg	leg	dancing
C)	tooth	tooth	biting
D)	nun	priest	sleeping
E)	ghost	ghost	always

51. You were a bad son, _____ you write.
You were a bad father, _____ you write.
You are alone, _____ you write.

A)	so	so	so
B)	of that	of that	of that
C)	but	but	but
D)	because	because	because
E)	and still	and still	and still

52. You were a bad son, so you write _____ .
You were a bad father, so you write _____ .
You are alone, so you write _____ .

A)	letters	letters	letters
B)	novels	stories	poetry
C)	badly	badly	badly
D)	your will	your will	your will
E)	a lot	a lot	a lot

53. You were a bad son, but _____ .
You were a bad father, but _____ .
You are alone, but _____ .

A)	people vote for you
	people vote for you
	people vote for you
B)	I love you
	I love you
	I love you
C)	I'm not your father
	I'm not your son
	that's not my problem
D)	you know it
	you know it
	you know it
E)	no one knows
	no one knows
	no one knows

54. You were a bad son, but _____ .
You were a bad father, but _____ .
You are alone, but _____ .

A) you're happy
   you're happy
   you're happy

B) it's so hard to be a son
   it's so hard to be a father
   we are all alone

C) a good soldier
   a good Christian
   Jesus is with you

D) your backhand is amazing
   you lent me sixty bucks
   man, you have a good time

E) your father died so long ago
   your son died so long ago
   you want to be alone

IV. SENTENCE ELIMINATION

In exercises 55 through 66, mark the answer that corresponds to the sentences or paragraphs that can be eliminated because they either do not add information or are unrelated to the rest of the text.

55.

(1) For years, no one came to visit my grave.

(2) I didn't expect anyone to, if I'm being honest.

(3) But today a woman came and left me flowers.

(4) Four red roses, two pink ones, and one white.

(5) I don't know who she is; I don't remember ever having met her.

(6) I don't think she knows I was a shitty person.

A) None

B) 2

C) 4

D) 5

E) 6

56.

(1) There are hamburgers in the refrigerator.

(2) There's some lettuce and mustard, too.

(3) I went to the beach with the kids.

(4) It's normal, they're my kids too.

(5) I'm afraid of you.

(6) And they're afraid of you too.

(7) And that, too, is normal.

A) None

B) 1 and 2

C) 2

D) 4

E) 7

57.

(1)   A curfew is a regulation prohibiting free circulation in public within a determined area.

(2)   It tends to be decreed in times of war or popular uprising.

(3)   The dictatorship imposed one in Santiago, Chile, from September 11, 1973, until January 2, 1987.

(4)   One summer evening my father went out walking with no destination in mind. It grew late, and he had to sleep at a friend's house.

(5)   They made love, she got pregnant, I was born.

A)   None

B)   5

C)   1, 2, and 3

D)   4 and 5

E)   2

58.

(1) I didn't want to talk about you, but it's inevitable.

(2) I'm talking about you right now. And you're reading this, and you know it's about you.

(3) Now I am words that you read and wish did not exist.

(4) I hate you.

(5) You would like to have the power of a censor.

(6) So no one else would ever read these words.

(7) I hate you.

(8) You ruined my life.

(9) Now I am words you cannot erase.

A) None

B) A

C) B

D) C

E) D

59.

(1) They found the breast cancer when she was sixty-five years old.

(2) They had to remove one of her breasts.

(3) Not long after that, the Alzheimer's started.

(4) She didn't recognize her children, or her grandchildren, not anyone.

(5) She didn't even recognize me.

(6) But she never forgot she was missing a breast.

A) None

B) 1

C) 2

D) 4

E) 5

60.

(1)   I only saw my mother's father three times in my life. It's unclear how many children he had: more than twenty, fewer than thirty, according to my mother's calculations.

(2)   The first time I saw him, he came to our house at night, when we were about to go to bed. He introduced us to Verónica, his youngest daughter. She was four or five years old, younger than I was.

(3)   "Say hi to your aunt Verito," he said to me and my sister. And then: "I've got your birthdays written down. I never forget my grandchildren."

(4)   They left around midnight, driving away in a Renoleta. It was cold. My mother had to lend Verito one of my sister's sweaters.

(5)   "They'll never give that sweater back," my mother told my sister over breakfast, containing her rage, or maybe just resigned.

(6)   The second time I saw him, some time later, was on my mother's birthday.

(7)   She was happy. I remember that absurd and true sentence: *He will always be my father.*

(8)   The last time I saw him was in a hospital. He shared a room with three other dying old men. My mom told me to go in and see him, to say good-bye.

(9)   I looked at the old men; all of them looked alike. I tried to recognize my mother's father, but I couldn't. I stared at them for a while, and then I left.

A) None
B) 3
C) 4 and 5
D) 7
E) 8 and 9

61.

(1) While we're making tea, Mariela tells me that when she was in school, there was a pregnant nun.

(2) I ask her when, where. "At Mater Dei. I was really little, in the fourth grade."

(3) Mariela's eyes are brown. For a second, I manage to picture her face when she was little.

(4) "They kept her hidden away, but we saw her once. They asked us to keep the secret."

(5) I ask her if they kept the secret. "I don't know about my friends," she replies, "but I did."

(6) "You're the first person I've told," she says.

(7) "Thirty years later?"

(8) "Yes, thirty," she says.

(9) She looks down at her hands. I also look at her hands.

(10) She pinches or caresses a breadcrumb. She lights a cigarette.

(11) "No," she says then. "Thirty-five."

A) None
B) 3
C) 9
D) 10
E) 11

62.

(1) In Chile, no one says hi to each other in elevators. You get in and pretend you don't see anyone, you pretend you're blind. And if you say hello, people look at you strangely, sometimes they don't even return the greeting. You share your fragility in silence, like a sacrifice.

(2) How hard would it be to say hello, you think, while the door opens on an in-between floor. There are already nine, ten people, and no one else can fit. Someone's headphones are playing a song that you know and like.

(3) It would be easier to embrace the woman standing there in front of you. What you and she share is the effort to avoid touching each other.

(4) You remember getting punished once when you were little, maybe eight years old: you'd been caught in the girls' bathroom swapping kisses with a little classmate. It wasn't the first time you and she had kissed each other. It was a game, a kind of dare. A teacher saw you, scolded you, brought you to the principal's office.

(5) Your punishment was to stand face-to-face, staring into each other's eyes and holding both hands, in the middle of the playground for the entire recess, while the other children yelled and teased you.

(6) She cried from the shame. You were on the verge of tears, but you kept your eyes on her face, you felt a kind of sad fire burning. Her name, the girl's, was Rocío.

(7) How long was that recess? Ten minutes, maybe fifteen. You never again spent fifteen minutes looking into another person's eyes.

(8) It would be easier to just embrace the stranger there in front of you. You are both looking down; you are taller than she is. You focus on her black, still-wet hair.

(9) The tangled strands of that long, straight hair: you think about the hair that you used to untangle, carefully, on certain mornings. You learned the technique. You know how to untangle the hair of another person.

(10) Now almost everyone has gotten off the elevator, and only she and you are left. With each new space that opens up, you take the opportunity to move apart. You could stand even farther apart, each of you clinging to your corner, but that would be demonstrating something. It would be the same as embracing.

(11) She gets off one floor before you. And it's strange and somehow horrible that when you see your body multiplied in the mirrors you feel the immense relief that you feel now.

(12) "In Chile, no one says hello to each other in elevators," you say that night, at a dinner with friends from abroad. "They don't in my country, either," everyone answers, maybe out of politeness. "No, really, in Chile no one says anything. People don't even look at each other in elevators," you insist.

(13) "Everyone fakes their absence. Old friends, enemies, or lovers could be in the same elevator and never know it."

(14)   You add generalizations about Chilean identity,
       rudimentary sociology. As you speak, you feel you are
       betraying something. You feel the sharp point, the
       weight of your imposture.

(15)   "In Chile, no one says hi to each other in elevators," you
       say again, like a refrain, at a dinner where everyone
       competes to be the best observer and to inhabit the
       worst country.

A)   None

B)   4, 5, 6, and 7

C)   8 and 9

D)   3, 4, 5, 6, 7, 8, 9, 10, and 11

E)   1, 2, 3, 8, 9, 10, 11, 12, 13, 14, and 15

63.

(1) I was his friend, I was his pal. I knew him. And it's not true what they say about him. Some things, sure, but not all of it. I care about what they say, it hurts. It's as if they were talking about me.

(2) It's true he thought fags were revolting, but he never fired anyone for being one. We all knew Salazar was batting for the other team—you only had to look at him. But he was lazy. My buddy fired him for being lazy, not for smoking pole.

(3) It isn't true that he mistreated the maid. There was a reason she kept working in his house so long. He used a bell to call her; sometimes he said "please" when he asked her for things. And every Christmas he gave her a brand-new, spotless uniform. And in February he brought her to the house in Frutillar. The old lady got a one-month vacation, all expenses paid.

(4) And what is the problem, if I may ask, with the bell? Do you mean to tell me it's better to call the maid by shouting at her?

(5) It's true he didn't like Mapuches, but it's just that these days you have to respect everyone. I mean, come on, you can't say anything—everything offends someone, and everyone's a victim. And my buddy was consistent. He said what he thought and that was his only sin.

(6) And what's the big deal with the Mapuches, anyway? They lost the war, same as the Peruvians. They lost, that's it. The Bolivians, too—now they go around crying

about how they don't have access to the sea, yapping on and on about maps. They're like little kids begging their parents for candy.

(7) Today you'll find people saying they didn't know about the disappearances, or the torture, or the murders. Of course they knew. My buddy knew, I knew, everyone did. How could we not? I remember years ago, we were in Rome, in a real swanky hotel, and this exiled guy comes over to us holding hands with a thin little redhead. I didn't much like the guy—I thought he was pretty dense and uppity—but my buddy ended up making friends with him, and later on they did some business together.

(8) My friend didn't discriminate against anyone. He could do business with any kind of person, he didn't care about race or creed or anything political. He didn't go around asking for favors. My buddy worked his whole life.

(9) Never, in forty-nine years of marriage, did he fool around on Tutú. He didn't even fuck that secretary, Vania, who drove him crazy flashing her panties at him all the time. I remember he told me, pretty desperate, that if he went to bed with Vania he wouldn't be able to look Father Carlos in the eye. Later we found out Father Carlos was a bigger lady-killer than any of us.

(10) I want to repeat this, because it goes to show the kind of moral stature my friend had: He never once fooled around on Tutú—he didn't even go to whores. He just didn't like them. To each his own, I guess.

(11) He didn't just donate to Legionaries of Christ—I think my friend was like a drug addict with donations. He was always helping out his neighbors, the guy was just sick with solidarity. And at the end of the year, he gave every one of his employees a gift basket that was nothing to sneeze at.

(12) Whatever they may say of him, it's easy enough to bad-mouth him now that he's dead. But I would like you all to know that my friend isn't all that dead, because he still has me, come what may. I'll always defend him. Always, buddy—always.

A) None

B) All

C) 4

D) 9 and 10

E) 2, 3, 4, 5, 6, 7, 8, 9, 10, and 11

64.

(1) They ask my name and I answer: Manuel Contreras. They ask me if I am Manuel Contreras. I say yes. They ask if I'm Manuel Contreras's son. I reply that I am Manuel Contreras.

(2) Once, I took the phone book and tore out the page with my name, our name. I counted twenty-two Manuel Contrerases in Santiago. I don't know what I was looking for: company for my misery, maybe. But then I stuck the page into the paper shredder. Having common first and last names hasn't done me any good.

(3) How does it feel to be the son of one of the biggest criminals in Chilean history? What do you feel when you think about your father, sentenced to more than three hundred years in jail? Can you sense the hate of the families your father destroyed?

(4) I can't answer these questions, the ones people always ask. With rage, but also with genuine curiosity. I guess it makes people curious.

(5) It makes me curious too. What does it feel like *not* to be the son of one of the biggest criminals in Chile's history? What does it feel like to think about how your father never killed anyone, never tortured anyone?

(6) I must say that my father is innocent. I should say it. I have to say it. I'm obliged to say it. My father will kill me if I don't say he is innocent. The children of murderers cannot kill the father.

(7)   I decided not to have children. I had my father to worry about. He's sick. His declining health is a public matter; it's been in all the papers.

(8)   When my father dies, then I can have a life and a son. He'll be Manuel Contreras's son. But I won't name him Manuel. I'll tell his mother to pick a different name. I don't want to be Manuel Contreras's father.

(9)   I've had enough just being Manuel Contreras's son. I don't want to be Manuel Contreras's father too. Better yet, let it be a girl.

(10) This is not me talking. Someone is talking for me. Someone who is faking my voice. My father will die soon. The person faking my voice knows this, and doesn't care.

(11) Maybe by the time the book this fucking voice faker is writing gets published, my father will be dead. And people will think that there is something true in what my fake voice says. Even though it isn't my voice. Though I would never really say what I'm saying now. Though no one has the right to speak for me. To make a fool of me. How easy it is to laugh at me. To blame me, to feel sorry for me. It has no literary merit.

(12) Clap for the writer, how ingenious. Clapping for him the way you have to clap for that kind of person. But clap him right in the face, with both hands, until you can't tell anymore where the blood is coming from.

(13) Now he's saying that I give orders, that I know how to torture. That I'm a chip off the old block. Now he says I'm telling you to stick a pitchfork up his ass.

(14) Now he's saying I don't have the right to challenge my
      destiny. That I'm one of the walking dead. That I'm
      saying things I'm not saying. That I even thank him for
      saying them for me. Now he's searching for words to
      tattoo on my chest using the biggest drill he has.

A) None
B) 9
C) 10, 11, and 12
D) 13 and 14
E) 14

65.

(1) With the money he won in the lottery, the old man decided to fulfill his lifelong dream, but since his lifelong dream had been to win the lottery, he didn't know what to do. In the meantime, he bought himself a Peugeot 505 and hired me to drive it.

(2) I went to pick him up one Saturday, and the plan was to hit the racetrack, but he was watching *Sábado Gigante* on TV and didn't feel like going out. He handed me a beer, and together we watched the segment "So You Think You Know Chile?" Don Francisco was traveling through Ancud and Castro, interviewing people who lived in some stilt houses, helping to cook a *curanto,* making a lot of effort to tug a Chilote wool cap over his extra-large head.

(3) "That's what we'll do," he told me, like he'd had a revelation: "We're going to tour Chile in the new car." I asked him why not travel the whole world, like Don Francisco himself in "The Spotlight Abroad." He replied that before seeing the world, one had to really see one's own country. I asked him where we would start, in the north or the south. "In the north, man, the north. What do you mean where do we start? This shit goes north to south."

(4) His opinion at the end of the trip: "Chile is a beautiful country. People are always complaining about the lack of freedom and the dictatorship and all that, but they don't realize that Chile is a beautiful country."

(5) I liked seeing my country too, but I don't remember that much. I drove like a zombie, to the beat of the old man's terrifying snores. Sometimes, out of the corner of my eye, I'd see the glint of drool in his open mouth. When he was awake, he didn't like to listen to music, just some cassettes with jokes by Coco Legrand. I came to hate Coco Legrand—his jokes, his voice, everything.

(6) I remember the cold near Los Vilos, where I smoked alone on the side of the road while five meters away, in the backseat of the car, the old man fondled two sad, big-titted whores. I remember when I woke him up on the beach at Cavancha and he thought I was a mugger. In Pelluhue a giant wave almost swallowed him, and I had to dive into the water in my underwear to save him. In Pichilemu he started to scold two pot smokers who were pacifists but still wanted to kick his ass. I also had to defend him in Talca, Angol, and Temuco.

(7) I remember the fear I felt in restaurants when the old man started to harass the waiters. My only moment of freedom was when he came down with some kind of stomach illness and had to be hospitalized in Puerto Montt. Those days I was fairly happy, but maybe only for a few hours, parked close to downtown, eating cheese empanadas while I listened to Los Angeles Negros and Los Prisioneros and the rain fell. And in Cañete. I was also happy in Cañete, but now I can't remember why.

(8) The old man paid me well, I have to admit. Afterward he went to travel around Europe and the United States, and we lost contact. Then one day he called me to ask if I knew anyone who could ghostwrite his autobiography for him. I told him I could do it myself, that I'd become a writer. It wasn't true, but I needed the money. He believed me.

(9) We agreed on a rate per word; the only thing he cared about was that the book was fat. I started to write his story. We met every morning and I listened to him. He was so presumptuous, such a poor observer, so arrogant, but I listened to him and took plenty of notes. "The Spanish are friendly," he might say to me, for example. "The Spanish from where?" I asked him. "What do you mean from where, asshole? The Spanish from Spain," he replied.

(10) I also had to interview his children, a man and a woman more or less my age, who had helpless faces and claimed to love and admire the old man, as did his ex-wife, a woman who always held a rosary in her right hand and who talked up a storm. It was clear they were lying, and I couldn't understand why they collaborated. Later, I learned that my boss had doubled their monthly allowances.

(11) One time I asked him, without any mean intention, if he thought the money had changed him. "You really ask some idiotic questions, kid. Of course it did," he replied. "Money changes everyone." Later I asked him for his opinion on Pinochet, which I already knew, I only wanted to make sure. It was 1987, one year after the

assassination attempt, a year before the referendum. I warned him that Chilean public opinion about Pinochet was going to change in the coming years whether he won or lost the referendum, and that maybe it wasn't such a good idea to come off as a fervent supporter of the dictator. "Let it be very clear in my book that I think Pinochet saved Chile, and that I want those mongoloids who tried to kill him to rot in hell," he answered.

(12) I asked him what he thought about Don Francisco. "Don Francisco was always my inspiration," he replied. "Don Francisco has traveled all over the world," I told him. "But no one invites Pinochet anywhere." I don't know why I said that to him. He sat there thinking. I warmed to the subject, and added that Don Francisco had shown us the Chile that Pinochet destroyed. "Go fuck your sister," he replied.

(13) I said nothing; I was used to that kind of humiliation. At the end of the day, I was only a ghostwriter. I worked for two more months and finished the book. Three hundred fifty-nine pages. I'm ashamed to confess that I was proud of some passages, that they struck me as well written, even eloquent. The book was garbage, but at least there were some parts that were, to my mind, inspired, and some elegant, almost baroque turns of phrase. He paid for a printing of five hundred copies. *My Journey Through the World and My Nation* was the title he chose.

(14) I thought I would never see him again. For fifteen years I heard nothing from him, until one day he called me

out of the blue. I asked him how he'd gotten my number. "A man has his ways," he said. He told me he was sick and could die soon, and he wanted to correct some things in the book for a second edition. I asked him if the first one had sold out. "I still have about a hundred books," he said, "but that's not enough." "What is it you want to correct?" I asked him. "Just the grammatical errors," answered that old piece of shit.

A)   None
B)   All
C)   Any
D)   A
E)   B

66.

(1)   I have six children: four boys and two girls. One of the girls is a lesbian, but I love her anyway because she's a good person. If I classify my children according to those terms, four are good and two are bad. One hundred percent of the girls: good. The boys: fifty percent bad.

(2)   Classified according to their ages: The oldest is forty-five years old and the youngest twenty-nine. According to their mothers: Eleonora (two boys and the two girls), Silvana (one), Daniela (the youngest).

(3)   I suggested names for all my children, but I only managed to get my way in two of the six cases.

(4)   Children of mine with moles on their faces: three. With a cleft chin: two. Long eyelashes: two.

(5)   Four of my children came to see me in the hospital when they removed my left kidney. The other two didn't, but they called.

(6)   Percentage of my children who have at some point said to me *I hate you*: 33.3.

(7)   Percentage of my children who declared their hate for me not with words but with action (a punch in the left eye): 16.6.

(8)   Children of mine who have asked my forgiveness: four.

(9)   Two of my sons learned to clip their fingernails and tie their shoes before they were three years old. I taught all of them to drive before they were eighteen.

(10)   Children of mine who have run over dogs: two. Children of mine who have run over people: one.

(11) Children of mine who work in the public sector: two. Private: two. Neither public nor private: two.

(12) Chilean presidential elections in the year 2013, my children's votes in the first round, with 100 percent reporting:

> Michelle Bachelet: two
> Marcel Claude: zero
> Marco Enríquez-Ominami: zero
> Tomás Jocelyn-Holt: zero
> Ricardo Israel: one
> Evelyn Matthei: one
> Roxana Miranda: one
> Franco Parisi: zero
> Alfredo Sfeir: one
> null votes: zero
> blank votes: zero

(13) My children's votes in the second round: three for Bachelet, one for Matthei, one drew a dick on the ballot, and one daughter didn't vote.

(14) Children of mine who have spent more than two consecutive nights in jail: zero.

(15) Children of mine dependent on drugs: five. Fluoxetine: two. Clonazepam: two. Lithium: one. Children of mine with flat feet: 100 percent. Children of mine with flat feet who refused to use insoles: two. Children of mine operated on for appendicitis: three.

(16) Five of my children are myopic and four of those also suffer from astigmatism.

(17) Of my five children with vision problems, two wanted surgery but couldn't afford it. Three use glasses, two prefer contacts. Of the three who wear glasses, two have thick rectangular frames. With the other one, it's no use: He has round frames, even though he knows people with round faces should wear square or rectangular frames.

(18) In general, when I have them all over for lunch, two of my children talk about politics and two about soccer. The oldest tends to relate his interminable amorous entanglements, and the other remains in absolute silence, just like when he was a boy, always looking at his plate as if he were rigorously analyzing the food.

(19) Children of mine who sometimes ask me for loans to buy medicine: two. To go to the track: one. To pay debts: two.

(20) Children of mine for whom I'd give my life: at least three.

(21) Children of mine who were planned: four.

(22) Children of mine who, in times of distress, tell me their problems: three. Children of mine to whom, in times of distress, I tell my problems: two.

(23) Children of mine who will be present at my funeral: six.

(24) Children of mine who will spit on my grave: one.

(25) Children of mine who have children: zero.

A) None

B) Any

C) All

D) 21

E) 25

V. READING COMPREHENSION

Next you will read three texts, each of them followed by questions or problems based on their content. Each question has five possible answers. Mark the one that you think is most appropriate.

TEXT #1

After so many study guides, so many practice and proficiency and achievement tests, it would have been impossible for us not to learn something, but we forgot everything almost right away and, I'm afraid, for good. The thing that we did learn, and to perfection—the thing we would remember for the rest of our lives—was how to cheat on tests. Here I could easily ad-lib an homage to the cheat sheet, all the test material reproduced in tiny but legible script on a minuscule bus ticket. But all that superb workmanship would have been worthless if we hadn't also had the necessary skill and audacity when the crucial moment came: the instant the teacher lowered his guard and the ten or twenty golden seconds began.

At our school in particular, which in theory was the strictest in Chile, it turned out that cheating was fairly easy, since many of the tests were multiple choice. We still had years to go before we'd take the Academic Aptitude Test and apply to university, but our teachers wanted to familiarize us right away with multiple-choice exercises, and although they designed up to four different versions of every test, we always found a way to pass information around. We didn't have to write anything or form opinions or develop any ideas of our own; all we had to do was play the game and guess the trick. Of course we studied, sometimes a lot, but it was never enough. I guess the idea was to lower our morale. Even if we did nothing but study, we knew there would always be two or three impossible questions. We didn't complain. We got the message: Cheating was just part of the deal.

I think that, thanks to our cheating, we were able to let go of some of our individualism and become a community. It's sad to put it this way, but cheating gave us a sense of solidarity. Every once in a while we suffered from guilt, from the feeling that we were frauds— especially when we looked ahead to the future—but in the end our indolence and defiance prevailed.

———

We didn't have to take religion—the grade didn't affect our averages— but getting out of it was a long bureaucratic process, and Mr. Segovia's classes were really fun. He'd go on and on in an endless soliloquy about any subject but religion; his favorite, in fact, was sex, and which teachers at our school he wanted to have it with. Every class we'd do a quick round of confessions: Each of us had to disclose a sin, and after listening to all forty-five—which ranged from *I kept the change* to *I want to grab my neighbor's tits* to *I jacked off during recess,* always a classic—the teacher would tell us that none of our sins were unforgivable.

I think it was Cordero who confessed one day that he had copied someone's answers in math, and since Segovia didn't react we all contributed variations of the same: *I copied on the Spanish test, on the science test, on the PE test* [laughter], and so on. Segovia, suppressing a smile, said that he forgave us, but that we had to make sure we didn't get caught, because that would really be unforgivable. Suddenly, though, he became serious. "If you are so dishonest at twelve," he said, "at forty you're going to be worse than the Covarrubias twins." We asked him who the Covarrubias twins were, and he looked as if he were going to tell us, but then he thought better of it. We kept at him, but he didn't want to explain. Later, we asked other teachers and even the guidance counselor, but no one wanted to tell us the story. The reasons were diffuse: It was a secret, a delicate subject, possibly something that would damage the school's impeccable reputation. We soon forgot the matter, in any case.

Five years later, it was 1993 and we were seniors. One day, when Cordero, Parraguez, little Carlos, and I were playing hooky, we ran into Mr. Segovia coming out of the Tarapacá pool hall. He wasn't a teacher anymore; he was a Metro conductor now, and it was his day off. He treated us to Coca-Colas, and ordered a shot of pisco for himself, though it was early to start drinking. It was then that he finally told us the story of the Covarrubias twins.

―――――

Covarrubias family tradition dictated that the firstborn son should be named Luis Antonio, but when Covarrubias senior found out that twins were on the way he decided to divide his name between them. During their first years of life, Luis and Antonio Covarrubias enjoyed—or suffered through—the excessively equal treatment that parents tend to give to twins: the same haircut, the same clothes, the same class in the same school.

When the twins were ten years old, Covarrubias senior installed a partition in their room, and he sawed cleanly through the old bunk bed to make two identical single beds. The idea was to give the twins a certain amount of privacy, but the change wasn't all that significant, because they still talked through the partition every night before falling asleep. They inhabited different hemispheres now, but it was a small planet.

When the twins were twelve they entered the National Institute, and that was their first real separation. Since the 720 incoming seventh-graders were distributed randomly, the twins were placed in different classes for the first time ever. They felt pretty lost in that school, which was so huge and impersonal, but they were strong and determined to persevere in their new lives. Despite the relentless barrage of looks and stupid jokes from their classmates ("I think I'm seeing double!"), they always met at lunch to eat together.

At the end of seventh grade, they had to choose between fine art and music; they both chose art, in the hope that they'd be placed together, but they were out of luck. At the end of eighth grade, when they had to choose between French and English, they planned to go with French, which, as the minority choice, would practically ensure that they'd be in the same class. But after a sermon from Covarrubias senior about the importance of knowing English in today's savage and competitive world, they gave in. Things went no better for them in their freshman and sophomore years, when students were grouped based on ranking, even though they both had good grades.

For their junior year, the twins chose a humanities focus, and finally they were placed together, in Class 3-F. Being classmates again after four years apart was fun and strange. Their physical similarity was still extraordinary, although acne had been cruel to Luis's face, and Antonio was showing signs of wanting to stand out: his hair was long, or what passed for long back then, and the layer of gel that plastered it back gave him a less conventional appearance than his brother's. Luis kept the classic cut, military style, his hair two fingers above his shirt collar as the regulations stipulated. Antonio also wore baggier pants and, defying the rules, often went to school in black sneakers instead of dress shoes.

The twins sat together during the first months of the school year. They protected and helped each other, though when they fought they seemed to hate each other, which, of course, is the most natural thing in the world: there are moments when we hate ourselves, and if we have someone in front of us who is almost exactly like us our hate is inevitably directed toward that person. But around the middle of the year, for no obvious reason, their fights became harsher, and at the same time, Antonio lost all interest in his studies. Luis's life, on the other hand, continued along its orderly path. He kept his record spotless, and his grades were very good; in fact, he was first in his class that year. Incredibly, his brother was last and would have to repeat the grade, and that was how the twins' paths diverged again.

There was only one school counselor for more than four thousand students, but he took an interest in the twins' case and called their parents in for a meeting. He offered the theory, not necessarily true, that Antonio had been driven by an unconscious desire (the counselor explained to them, quickly and accurately, exactly what the unconscious was) not to be in the same class as his brother.

Luis sailed through his senior year with excellent grades, and got outstanding scores on all the university entrance exams, especially History of Chile and Social Studies, on which he got nearly the highest scores in the nation. He entered the University of Chile to study law, on a full scholarship.

———

The twins were never as distant from each other as they were during Luis's first months in college. Antonio was jealous when he saw his brother leaving for the university, free now of his uniform, while he was still stuck in high school. Some mornings their schedules coincided, but thanks to a tacit and elegant agreement—some version, perhaps, of the famous twin telepathy—they never boarded the same bus.

They avoided each other, barely greeting one another, though they knew that their estrangement couldn't last forever. One night, when Luis was already in his second semester of law, Antonio started talking to him again through the partition. "How's college?" he asked.

"In what sense?"

"The girls," Antonio clarified.

"Oh, there are some really hot girls," Luis replied, trying not to sound boastful.

"Yeah, I know there are girls, but how do you do it?"

"How do we do what?" said Luis, who, deep down, knew exactly what his brother was asking.

"How do you fart with girls around?"

"Well, you just have to hold it in," Luis answered.

They spent that night, as they had when they were children, talking and laughing while they competed with their farts and burps, and from then on they were once again inseparable. They kept up the illusion of independence, especially from Monday to Friday, but on weekends they always went out together, matched each other drink for drink, and played tricks switching places, taking advantage of the fact that, thanks to Luis's newly long hair and now-clear skin, their physical resemblance was once again almost absolute.

Antonio's academic performance had improved a great deal, but he still wasn't a model student, and toward the end of his senior year he began to get anxious. Though he felt prepared for the aptitude test, he wasn't sure that he would be able to score high enough to study law at the University of Chile like his brother. The idea was Antonio's, naturally, but Luis accepted right away, with no blackmail or stipulations, and without an ounce of fear, since at no point did he consider it possible that they would be found out. In December of that year, Luis Covarrubias registered, presenting his brother Antonio's ID card, to take the test for the second time, and he gave it his all. He tried so hard that he got even better scores than he had the year before: in fact, he received the nation's highest score on the Social Studies test.

"But none of us have twin brothers," Cordero said that afternoon, when Segovia finished his story. It may have been drizzling or raining, I don't remember, but I know that the teacher was wearing a blue raincoat. He got up to buy cigarettes, and when he came back to our table he stayed on his feet, maybe to reestablish a protocol that had been lost: the teacher stands, the students sit. "You'll still come out ahead," he told us. "You don't know how privileged you are."

"Because we go to the National Institute?" I asked.

He puffed anxiously on his cigarette, perhaps already somewhat drunk, and he was silent for so long that it was no longer necessary to answer, but then an answer came. "The National Institute is rotten, but the world is rotten," he said. "They prepared you for this, for a world where everyone fucks everyone over. You'll do well on the test, very well, don't worry—you weren't educated, you were trained." It sounded aggressive, but there was no contempt in his tone, or, at least, none directed at us.

We were quiet; it was late by then, almost nighttime. He sat down looking absorbed, thoughtful. "I didn't get a high score," he said, when it seemed there wouldn't be any more words. "I was the best in my class, in my whole school. I never cheated on an exam, but

I bombed the aptitude test, so I had to major in religious education. I didn't even believe in God."

I asked him if now, as a Metro conductor, he earned more money. "Twice as much," he replied. I asked him if he believed in God now, and he answered that yes, now more than ever, he believed in God. I'll never forget his gesture then: with a lit cigarette between his index and middle fingers, he looked at the back of his hand as if searching for his veins, and then he turned it over, as if to make sure that his life, head, and heart lines were still there.

We said good-bye as if we were or had once been friends. He went into the cinema, and we headed down Bulnes toward Parque Almagro to smoke a few joints.

———

I never heard anything more about Segovia. Sometimes on the Metro, when I get into the first car, I look toward the conductor's booth and imagine that our teacher is in there, pressing buttons and yawning. As for the Covarrubias twins, they've gained a certain amount of fame, and as I understand it, they never separated again. They became identical lawyers; I hear it's hard to tell which is the more brilliant and which the more corrupt. They have a firm in Vitacura, and they charge the same rate. They charge what such good service is worth: a lot.

Exercises:

67. According to the text, the Covarrubias twins' experience in their new school:

    (A) Marked their final break with the values their parents had instilled in them.

    (B) Was traumatic, because it forced them to make rash decisions and separated them for good.

    (C) Gradually shaped them into productive individuals who contributed to Chilean society.

    (D) Transformed two good and supportive brothers into unscrupulous sons of bitches.

    (E) Marked the start of a difficult period, from which they emerged stronger and ready to compete in this ruthless and materialistic world.

68. The best title for this story would be:

    (A) "How to Train Your Twin"

    (B) "To Sir, with Love"

    (C) "Me and My Shadow"

    (D) "Against Lawyers"

    (E) "Against Twin Lawyers"

69. Regarding multiple-choice tests, the author affirms that:

I. They were regularly used at that particular school in order to prepare students for the university entrance exams.

II. It was easier to cheat on those tests, any way you looked at it.

III. They did not require you to develop your own thinking.

IV. With multiple-choice tests, the teachers didn't have to make themselves sick in the head by grading all weekend long.

V. The correct choice is almost always D.

(A) I and II

(B) I, III, and V

(C) II and V

(D) I, II, and III

(E) I, II, and IV

70. The fact that Mr. Luis Antonio Covarrubias divided his name between his twin sons indicates that he was:

(A) Innovative

(B) Ingenious

(C) Unbiased

(D) Masonic

(E) Moronic

71. One can infer from the text that the teachers at the school:

   (A) Were mediocre and cruel, because they adhered unquestioningly to a rotten educational model.
   (B) Were cruel and severe: they liked to torture the students by overloading them with homework.
   (C) Were deadened by sadness, because they got paid shit.
   (D) Were cruel and severe, because they were sad. Everyone was sad back then.
   (E) The kid next to me marked C, so I'm going to mark C as well.

72. From this text, one infers that:

   (A) The students cheated on tests because they lived under a dictatorship, and that justified everything.
   (B) Cheating on tests isn't so bad as long as you're smart about it.
   (C) Cheating on tests is part of the learning process for any human being.
   (D) The students with the worst scores on the university entrance exams often become religion teachers.
   (E) Religion teachers are fun, but they don't necessarily believe in God.

73. The purpose of this story is:

(A) To suggest a possible work opportunity for Chilean students who perform well academically but are poor (there aren't many, but they do exist): they could take tests for students who are lazy and rich.

(B) To expose security problems in the administration of the university entrance exams, and to promote a business venture related to biometric readings, or some other system for definitively verifying the identities of students

(C) To promote an expensive law firm. And to entertain.

(D) To legitimate the experience of a generation that could be summed up as "a bunch of cheaters." And to entertain.

(E) To erase the wounds of the past.

74. Which of Mr. Segovia's following statements is, in your opinion, true?

(A) You weren't educated, you were trained.

(B) You weren't educated, you were trained.

(C) You weren't educated, you were trained.

(D) You weren't educated, you were trained.

(E) You weren't educated, you were trained.

TEXT #2

I suppose we were happy on my wedding day, though it's hard for me to imagine it now; I can't fathom how during such a bitter time any sort of happiness was possible. This was September 2000, fourteen years ago, which is a lot of time: 168 months, more than five thousand days.

The party was memorable, that's for sure, especially after that soulless, torturous ceremony in our apartment. We'd done a thorough cleaning the night before, but I think our relatives still whispered about us as they left, because there's no denying that those threadbare armchairs and the wine-stained walls and carpeting didn't give the impression of a place that was fit for a wedding.

The bride—of course I remember her name, though I think eventually I'll forget it, someday I will even forget her name—looked lovely, but my parents just couldn't understand why she would wear a black dress. I wore a gray suit so shiny and shabby that an uncle of the bride's said I looked more like an office gofer than a groom. It was a classist and stupid comment, but it was also true, because that was precisely the suit I'd worn when I worked as an office gofer. I still associate it, more than with the wedding, with those endless days I spent walking around downtown or waiting in line at some bank, with humiliatingly short hair and a cornflower blue tie that could never be loosened enough.

Luckily, the official from the civil registrar left straightaway, and after the champagne and modest hors d'oeuvres—I remember with shame that the potato chips were all crushed—we had a long lunch, and we even had time to take a nap and change clothes before our friends began to arrive, bringing, as we'd requested, generous alcoholic contributions instead of gifts. There was so much booze that pretty soon we were sure we wouldn't be able to drink it all, and because we were high that seemed like a problem. We debated the issue for a long time, although (since we were high) maybe it wasn't really that long.

Then Farra carried in an enormous, empty twenty-five-liter drum he had in his house for some reason, and we started to fill it up, dumping bottles in haphazardly while we half-danced, half-shouted. It was a risky bet, but the concoction—that's what we called it, we thought the word was funny—turned out to be delectable. How I would love to go back to the year 2000 and record the exact combination that led to that unexpected and delicious drink. I'd like to know exactly how many bottles or boxes of red and how many of white went in, what was the dosage of pisco, of vodka, of whiskey, tequila, gin, whatever. I remember there was also Campari, and anise, mint, and gold liqueurs, some scoops of ice cream, and even some powdered juice in that unrepeatable jug.

The next thing I remember is that we woke up sprawled in the living room, not just the bride and me but a ton of other people, some of whom I'd never even met, though I don't know if they were crashing the party or were distant cousins of the bride, who had—I discovered then—an astonishing number of distant cousins. It was maybe ten in the morning. We were all having trouble stringing words together, but I wanted to try out the ultramodern coffeemaker my sister had given us, so I brewed several liters of coffee and little by little we shook off our sleep. I went to the big bathroom—the small one was covered in vomit—and I saw my friend Maite sleeping in the tub, lolling in an unlikely position, though she looked pretty comfortable, her right cheek pressed against the ceramic as if it were an enviable feather pillow. I woke her up and offered her a cup of coffee, but she opted for a beer instead to keep the hangover at bay.

Later, at around one in the afternoon, Farra switched on a camera he'd brought with him to film the party but had only just remembered. I was flopped in a corner of the room, drinking my zillionth coffee while the bride dozed against my chest. "Tell me, how does it feel?" Farra questioned me, in the tone of an overenthusiastic small-town reporter.

"To be married?" I asked him.

"No—to be married in a country where you can't get divorced." I told him not to be an ass, but he kept going. He told me his interest was genuine. I didn't want to look at him, but he went right on filming me. "Why all the celebration," he insisted, not letting up, "when you're just going to separate in a couple of years? You'll call me yourself. You'll come see me in my office, begging me to process your annulment."

"No," I answered, uncomfortable.

Then the bride sat up and rubbed her immense green eyes, caressed my hair, smiled at Farra, and said lightly, as if she'd spent some time thinking about the matter, that as long as divorce wasn't legal in Chile, we wouldn't separate. And then I added, looking defiantly into the camera: "We will stay married in protest, even if we hate each other."

She hugged me, we kissed, and she said that we wanted to go down in the nation's history as the first Chilean couple to get divorced. "It's a stupendous law. We recommend that everyone get divorced now," I said, playing along, and she, looking at the camera too, now with unanimous laughter in the background, seconded the opinion: "Yes, it's an absolutely commendable law."

"Chile is one of the few countries in the world where divorce isn't legal," someone said.

"It's the only one," someone else clarified.

"No, there are still a few left," said another.

"In Chile," Farra continued, "the divorce law will never pass. They've been arguing over it for years and nothing's happened, especially with the whole rotten Catholic lobby against it. They even said they'd excommunicate any representatives on the right who voted for it. So the world will just go right on laughing at us." Then someone said that the divorce law was not the most urgent thing to be fixed in the country, and then that sluggish conversation turned into a collective debate. As if we were filling up another drum, this time with our complaints or our wishes, almost all of us had something to contribute: the urgent thing is for Pinochet to go to jail, to go to trial, to go to hell, the urgent thing is to find the bodies of the disappeared, the urgent thing is education. The really urgent thing, said one guy, is to teach Mapudungún in schools, and someone asked him if he was, by chance, Mapuche ("more or less," he replied). The urgent thing is health care, said someone else, and then came another, then others: the urgent thing is to fight capitalism, the urgent thing is for Colo-Colo to win the Copa Libertadores again, the urgent thing is to fuck Opus Dei up, the urgent thing is to kick Iván Moreira's ass. The urgent thing is the war on drugs, added one of the bride's distant cousins, getting everyone's attention, but right away he clarified that it was a joke.

"We live in the country of waiting," the poet said then. There were several poets at the party, but he was the only one who deserved the title, because he tended to talk like a poet. More precisely, he spoke in the unmistakable tone of a drunk poet, of a drunk Chilean poet, of a young, drunk, Chilean poet: "We live in the country of waiting; we live in wait for something. Chile is one giant waiting room, and we will all die waiting for our number to be called."

"What number?" someone asked.

"The number they give you in waiting rooms, dumb-ass," someone said. Then there was complete silence, and I took the opportunity to close my eyes, but I opened them again right away because everything was spinning.

"Goddamn, you talk nice," Maite told the poet then. "I could really be into you. The only problem is how small your dick is."

"And how do you know that?" asked the poet, and she confessed she had spent hours hiding in the bathtub, looking at the penises of the men who went to piss. Then the poet said, with a slight but convincing scientific intonation, that the size of the penis when pissing was not representative of the penis in an erect state, and there was a general murmur of approval.

"Let's see, then—show it to me erect," said Maite, all in.

"I can't," said the poet. "I'm too drunk to get it up. You can try going down on me if you want, but I'm sure I won't get hard." They went to the bathroom or to the poet's house, I don't remember.

"I'm sorry," Farra said to us later, I suppose regretfully, the camera now turned off. "I don't want you two to separate. But if one day you do, you know you can count on me, both of you: I'll handle the separation for free." I don't know if we smiled at him—now I think we did, but it must have been a bitter smile. The guests left one by one, and it was night by the time we were alone. We collapsed into bed and slept for about twelve hours straight, our arms around each other. We always slept in an embrace. We loved each other, of course we did. We loved each other.

Two years later, just as Farra had foretold, we went to see him in his office. The divorce law was still stalled in Congress; it was said that its approval was imminent, but Farra told us that in no way was it worth waiting for. He even thought that afterward, once it passed, divorce would be more expensive than annulment. He explained the process to us. We'd already known that the judgment of nullity was ridiculous, but when we learned the details, it also struck us as immoral. We had to declare that neither she nor I had lived at the addresses that appeared on our marriage contract, and we had to find some witnesses who would attest to it.

"How idiotic," I told the bride that afternoon, at a café on Agustinas. "How pathetic, how shameful to be a judge who listens to someone lie and pretends not to know they're lying."

"Chile is idiotic," she said, and I think that was the last time the two of us were in total agreement on something. We didn't want to get an annulment, but it was fitting, in some sense. Now that I think about it, the best way to summarize our story together would be that I gradually annulled her and she me, until finally we were both entirely annulled.

In May 2004, Chile became the penultimate country in the world to legalize divorce, but the bride and I had already gotten our annulment. Maite and the poet, who were a couple by then, were going to be our witnesses, but at the last minute the poet backed out and I had to ask the favor of the woman whom, a few years later, I married. I'm not going to tell that story here; it's enough to say that with her, things were completely different. With her, things worked out: she and I were able, finally, to divorce.

Exercises:

75. The general tone of this story is:

    A) Melancholic
    B) Comic
    C) Parodic
    D) Sarcastic
    E) Nostalgic

76. What is the worst title for this story—the one that would reach the widest possible audience?

    A) "Five Thousand and One Nights"
    B) "Two Years of Solitude"
    C) "Fourteen Years of Solitude"
    D) "Two Weddings and No Funeral"
    E) "The Labyrinth of Nullity"

77. In your opinion, who is the victim and who is the victimizer, respectively, in this story?

    A) The bride / the groom
    B) The poet / Maite
    C) Chile / Chile
    D) Liver / concoction
    E) Liquor / beer

78. According to the text, at the beginning of the twenty-first century the nation of Chile was:

A) Conservative in its morality and liberal in its economy.

B) Conservative in its inebriety and artificial in all things holy.

C) Innovative in its levity and literal in its tragedy.

D) Aggressive in its religiosity and conjugal in its wizardry.

E) Exhaustive in its chicanery and indecisive in its celerity.

79. The narrator doesn't mention the bride's name because:

A) He wants to protect her. Moreover, he knows that he doesn't have the right to name her, to expose her. That fear of naming her, in any case, is so 1990s.

B) He wants to protect the woman's identity because he's afraid she might sue him.

C) He says he'll eventually forget the woman's name, but maybe he's already forgotten it. Or maybe he's still in love with her. There's someone I'm trying so hard to forget. Don't you want to forget someone too?

D) He's a misogynist. And a sexist. He's so vain, he probably thinks the story is about him. Doesn't he? Doesn't he?

E) If you can't be with the one you love, honey, love the one you're with.

80. According to the text, the divorce law wasn't passed sooner in Chile because:

A) The Catholic Church lobbied intensely against it, even threatening to excommunicate the congresspeople who supported the bill.

B) There were other priorities in the areas of health, education, and justice.

C) The priority was to indefinitely put off any reform that might put the country's stability at risk.

D) The priority was to put off indefinitely any reform that might put at risk the interests of corporations and the impunity of those responsible for crimes during the dictatorship, including, of course, Pinochet. In this context, the divorce law was hardly a question of values, and even the right-wing leaders—many of whom "annulled" and remarried—knew it was disgraceful that Chile still hadn't legalized divorce, but they put the matter off until they needed a powerful distraction that would neutralize the public outcry for justice and radical reforms.

E) A much better system existed: annulment. Because when a couple separates, what we really want is to believe that we were never married, that the person with whom we wanted to share our lives never existed. Nullity was the best way to erase the unerasable.

81. Which of the following famous phrases best reflects the meaning of the text?

    A)   "Marriage is the chief cause of divorce." (Groucho Marx)

    B)   "A marriage is no amusement but a solemn act, and generally a sad one." (Queen Victoria)

    C)   "A second marriage is the triumph of hope over experience." (Samuel Johnson)

    D)   "Unable to suppress love, the Church wanted at least to disinfect it, and it created marriage." (Charles Baudelaire)

    E)   "Marriage is the only adventure open to the cowardly." (Voltaire)

82. The end of this story is, without a doubt:

    I.   Sad

    II.   Heavy

    III.   Ironic

    IV.   Abrupt

    V.   Immoral

    VI.   Realistic

    VII. Funny

    VIII. Absurd

    IX.   Implausible

    X.   Legalistic

    XI.   Bad

    XII. It's a happy ending, in its own way.

A) I, II, and IV
B) X
C) All of the above
D) VIII and XI
E) XII

TEXT #3

Pay no mind, my son, to what I tell you; pay me no mind at all. I hope that time, in your memory, will mitigate my shouting, my inappropriate remarks, and my stupid jokes. I hope that time will erase almost all of my words, and preserve only the warm, still murmur of love. I hope that very soon they invent a remote control that lets you lower my volume, pause me, fast-forward through unpleasant scenes, or rewind very quickly to happy days. So you can experience whenever you want the freedom of acting without my vigilance, the immense pleasure of trying out a life without me. And you could even decide, for example, if it were necessary, to erase me. I don't mean erase these words, which in and of themselves are liquid, perishable. Rather, erase me completely, as if I'd never existed.

I know that is impossible.

That's what life consists of, I'm afraid: erasing and being erased. We were on the verge of erasing you, as you may already know or suspect. We didn't want to have a child. The thing is, we were still someone's children then. So much so that the possibility of being parents ourselves seemed terribly distant. We also knew in advance that we were going to separate. For us love was an incident, an accident, a practice—best-case scenario, a high-risk sport.

A little before we found out about the pregnancy, we had considered breaking up. Maybe it will come as a shock to learn that the reason for our fights had been the dilemma of whether or not to have a dog. At first she wanted one, but I thought it was too much responsibility. Then I was the one who wanted it and she argued we were fine as we were, that we had to establish ourselves as a couple before getting a dog. In the end we agreed: we weren't sure we'd be able to take good care of it, or would have the patience and discipline necessary to take it for walks every day, be sure its dish was always full of food, apply flea repellent every month.

We thought we were too young to take on the responsibility of a dog, but we weren't really so young: I was twenty-four, same as your mother. At that age, my father already had two children. The younger one, four years old, was me. But in my generation—I know you hate that word—having children was something we only began to think about at thirty or thirty-five, if we ever started thinking about it. Anyway, I don't know if it's any consolation, but when we found out about the pregnancy we never considered the possibility of an abortion. I mean, we thought about it, we asked about prices at clandestine clinics, we even went to one of them, but we didn't seriously consider it. It would be inexact to say that we changed our minds, because, as I've said, it was one idea among many, but it wasn't the primary one.

The day you were born was the happiest day of my life, but I was so nervous I don't know if *happiness* is really the best word to describe what I felt. I think it is my obligation to tell you, in spite of the absolute love I have always felt for you, in spite of how much you have brightened my life, and I assume your mother's as well—I haven't seen her in around ten years now, but I'm sure that for her as well, you have been a constant source of happiness—in spite of all that, I have to tell you that during the eighteen years you've now been alive, I've never stopped wondering what my life would have been like if you had never been born.

It's an overwhelming thought, an exit that leads to the darkest of nights, to the most complete blackness, but also to shadow and sometimes, slowly, toward something like a clearing in the woods. These fantasies are normal, but it's not so common for parents to confess them. For example, over the years I have thought thousands of times that if you hadn't been born I would have needed less money, or could have disappeared for weeks on end without worrying about anyone. I could have prolonged my youth for several more years. I could have even killed myself. I mean, the first consequence of your birth was that from then on, I could never kill myself. When some friend of mine who doesn't have kids talks to me about his little wounds where, after languidly digging around in them, he's found infinite desperation and anguish, I don't say what I really think, which is this: Why don't you just kill yourself?

I don't know if my life would make sense without you. I don't think my life has any meaning other than to be with you.

Everyone gets erased—life consists of meeting people whom first you love and then you erase—but you can't erase children, you can't erase parents. I know you've tried to erase me, and you couldn't. I know I have existed, for you, in excess. That I have also existed in absence. When I wasn't there, when I went weeks without seeing you that year I spent out of Chile, for example: even then I existed too much, because I wasn't there but my absence was. That's why I think it is only fair to tell you that I have also tried to erase you. All parents fantasize about those irresponsible lives, about eternal youth, sudden heroism. It's the distortion of something we used to say, trying to imbue the words with a certain philosophical density: why bring children into a shitty world?

Our parents didn't think that, they believed in love automatically, they married very young and they were unhappy, but not so much more than we were. They worked a ton and they didn't even try to associate work with any kind of happiness, so their suffering was more concrete. Plus, they believed in God and they made us believe in God. That's why we ate our food, that's why we did our homework, that's why it was hard for us, at night, to fall asleep: because God was watching us.

But we soon forgot God. We dismissed him as one more character from the stories of our childhood. We didn't want to be like our parents. We wanted, at most, to have puppies, kittens, and tortoises, even parrots, although the wish to have something as nasty as a parrot has always been incomprehensible to me. We wanted to be children without children, which was the way to remain children forever and thus to blame our parents for everything. What we received when you were born was a little animal that was too alive, and also an excuse, the perfect alibi, a mantra, a multipurpose sentence: *I have a son.* I was never so motivated as in those first years to ask for raises, to avoid unnecessary commitments, to stop smoking and drinking so much or to smoke and drink like crazy, because in our language the phrase *I have a son* meant, in a not-so-tacit way, *I have a problem.* I must admit I knew perfectly well how to add seductive nuances to that phrase: *I have a son* meant, in some cases, *I'm a serious man, I have lived, I'm responsible, I have a history, so go to bed with me.* And the next morning, if I didn't want to stay, or want her to stay for breakfast: *Sorry, I have to go, you have to go, I have a son.*

Except for those videos your mother got it into her head to show you—I don't know whether for better or worse—I understand you don't have any memory of our life when the three of us were together. When you were seven years old you told me that some of your classmates lived with their father and mother and you thought that was boring, because they only had one house. At the time I laughed, I wanted to interpret it literally, but I know there was pain there, a recrimination, though maybe an unconscious one. But in the end, almost all of your classmates had divorced parents. And even so I feel that the abyss separating you and me is deeper and more irrevocable than the abyss that always separates children from their parents.

We never told you why we separated. I'm going to tell you now. The reason for our separation was Cosmo. Yes, Cosmo. It's a sad story. You have to understand that we were going to separate anyway; for years we'd been looking for reasons, and of course if you hadn't been born we would have separated much earlier. That afternoon I was furious with you but also unsure: you were barely three years old but you were very self-determined, and when you saw that poor abandoned puppy in the garbage bin on the corner, you picked him up and went right on walking. I told you we couldn't keep him, but there was no way to make you understand. I was amazed that there was no crying—you were a crier but you didn't cry then, which in some way revealed to me that you existed, that I couldn't fool you anymore. You stroked the dog and named him Cosmo, and as we walked home I felt overpowered. I can think of no other word: overpowered. I understood while we were walking that right then a struggle was beginning, and it was one I would lose a thousand times: the struggle that perhaps now, with these words, I'm definitively losing.

I opened the door convinced, willing to respect your decision, and at first your mother agreed. But that night, after some hours of false harmony, the escalation of mutual accusations began, until finally she said: *We already have one*. I asked how she could possibly talk about you as a pet. She went quiet, and I think I felt the fanfare of triumph, but then, after arguing about many other things that I don't remember, when we'd already accepted that we would keep Cosmo, I was the one who said exactly the same words, meaning the same thing: *we already have one*.

Neither your mother nor I were talking about you. We were talking about you, but only to hurt each other through you. We competed for the scepter of who loved you more. For years we had agreed that we did not agree. And that night I left the house. And not long afterward your mother brought Cosmo to my apartment, which ended up being good because, like all children, some weekends you didn't want to be with your dad, but your mother reminded you that you had to take care of Cosmo. You didn't come to see me, you came to see Cosmo.

Sometimes I think your mother and I should get together and ask your forgiveness. Or take ayahuasca and ask your forgiveness. But it would be better if they would invent, once and for all, that remote control, so you can fast-forward and rewind, so you can pause, so you can erase some scenes of the life we have given you. You can't erase us, but maybe there are some erasable people: your sporadic stepmothers, most of your stepfathers, and your teachers. So you can erase all of the bad ones, you can erase everyone who has hurt you. And you can manipulate and distort and freeze the images of us, the ones who have hurt you but whom you can't erase. So you can watch us in slow motion, or normal or sped up. Or maybe you won't see us at all, but you'll know we are there, dragging out ever longer the absurd film of life.

Exercises:

83. The comparison between having a child and having a pet aims to show:

I. The contradictions of a generation that, under the pretext of a pessimistic view of the world, chose to have pets rather than children.

II. The importance of passing laws regarding responsible pet ownership.

III. The importance of passing laws regarding responsible child ownership.

A) I and III
B) I and II
C) I
D) II
E) III

84. A more or less good title for the text you have just read is:

A) "My Generation" (The Who)
B) "Generación de Mierda" (Los Prisioneros)
C) "I Wanna Be Your Dog" (the Stooges)
D) "Father and Son" (the Cat Stevens song that at one point says, "Look at me, I am old, but I'm happy," but it doesn't sound like he's happy; in fact it's the saddest moment of the whole song)

E) "They Fuck You Up, Your Mum and Dad" (Philip Larkin). Really, almost any line from that poem would work.

85. Ayahuasca is mentioned in the text to:

A) Give the narrative an ethnic touch.

B) There is no concrete reason to talk about ayahuasca. It's a whim of the author.

C) Encourage drug abuse.

D) Empathize with young people who have maybe already tried marijuana, cocaine, and/or crack and are now debating between going the natural, organic route or turning to chemical shortcuts. At this crossroads, the text intends, wisely, to promote ayahuasca, which is the doorway to self-knowledge.

E) Ayahuasca is considered useful in the field of psychiatry, especially in the treatment of depression, anxiety, and schizophrenia. We can't rule out that the author of this text could be suffering from one or more of these illnesses.

86. Which of the following characters in the story do you relate to?

A) None of them.

B) The son, obviously.

C) The father.

D) The father's parents and the mother. But also the father a little, and the son. And that poor little puppy, Cosmo.

E) The mother, because I also got pregnant at that age, but I had an abortion. I regretted it so many times, and every time I think of it I get depressed. But after reading this story I think it may not have been such a bad decision.

87. Which of the following options is the best characterization of the father?

A) He is an honest and brave man, or maybe someone who, after making many mistakes, understands that it is necessary to be completely honest. He tries to tell his son the truth, and damn if it isn't hard to tell the truth.

B) He is a pathetic man waiting to die.

C) He is a sensitive man, willing to give everything for his son, but he's just a hair unbalanced. You can tell he's trying to do something. It's unclear what, but he's definitely trying to do something.

D) He is an unreasonable old man who seems to be worried about his son, but who doesn't consider his words. He seems to regret the education he has given his son, and he thinks he can solve everything by sending him a letter.

E) He is a demented guy and an exhibitionist guy who crosses the line that should always exist between fathers and sons on the pretext of asking forgiveness. I'm not sure if his cruelty is voluntary, but I am sure that it is unnecessary.

88. In your opinion, which e-mail folder would be the most appropriate for a text like this one?

A) Sent messages
B) Drafts
C) Inbox
D) Spam
E) Unsent messages

89. After reading this text, you would rather:

A) Not have read it.
B) Not have children.
C) Have many children.
D) Not have a father.
E) Have a parrot.

90. If you were the addressee of this letter, your reaction would be:

A) I'm not really sure. As I was reading, I thought that this father could perfectly well be mine. If my old man wrote me something like this, I think I would feel sorry for him, which is what sometimes, maybe too often, I do feel. That pity would get mixed in with other, indeterminate feelings, which I would have to analyze in detail, preferably in therapy, but with a good therapist, not a quack like that clown I went to last year, who, when I told him I was desperate, recommended that I cry, and when I replied that yes, when I was desperate I cried, told me I shouldn't be worried then. In our last session he recommended that I try to face life with a little more "positivism."

B) I would hug him and thank him sincerely. I would take the chance to tell him that last week, Marce and I went to a clandestine clinic and we were really nervous, but everything worked out. It would be the perfect moment to tell him that we paid for the abortion by selling some of my mother's necklaces, and also the big-screen TV, the juicer, and the microwave, so I had to pretend we'd been robbed, and for a minute I was scared to death, because the cops came and I thought they were going to realize the robbery was fake. I'd also tell him that I got the rest of the money by selling his first editions of Chilean poetry in an antique bookstore on Manuel Montt, so he shouldn't keep looking for them :-)

C) If only my father were still alive. Maybe if he were alive and he told me all that, I'd be happy. I would think: He's an asshole, but he's alive. But my father wasn't an asshole and he never would have told me something like that; he never would have written me a letter like that. Another thing, while I have the chance, about dogs and cats: parents want their children to be dogs, but children are always cats. Parents want to domesticate their children, but children are like cats: you can't domesticate them.

D) I don't know how I would react. What kind of father says those things to his son? It'd be better if I punched him. Better to beat the shit out of him. Was there really no other way to let out his frustrations than to attack his son? Was it really necessary to tell him he wasn't wanted? I'm pretty sure my parents didn't want me either, but I'd rather not know. Why do we have to know so many things about our parents? Why can't parents just keep their mouths shut?

E)   I would give my father a parrot, but first I would teach it to say: *fucking asshole, fucking asshole, fucking asshole.*

	A B C D E		A B C D E		A B C D E
1	○○○○○	31	○○○○○	61	○○○○○
2	○○○○○	32	○○○○○	62	○○○○○
3	○○○○○	33	○○○○○	63	○○○○○
4	○○○○○	34	○○○○○	64	○○○○○
5	○○○○○	35	○○○○○	65	○○○○○
6	○○○○○	36	○○○○○	66	○○○○○
7	○○○○○	37	○○○○○	67	○○○○○
8	○○○○○	38	○○○○○	68	○○○○○
9	○○○○○	39	○○○○○	69	○○○○○
10	○○○○○	40	○○○○○	70	○○○○○
11	○○○○○	41	○○○○○	71	○○○○○
12	○○○○○	42	○○○○○	72	○○○○○
13	○○○○○	43	○○○○○	73	○○○○○
14	○○○○○	44	○○○○○	74	○○○○○
15	○○○○○	45	○○○○○	75	○○○○○
16	○○○○○	46	○○○○○	76	○○○○○
17	○○○○○	47	○○○○○	77	○○○○○
18	○○○○○	48	○○○○○	78	○○○○○
19	○○○○○	49	○○○○○	79	○○○○○
20	○○○○○	50	○○○○○	80	○○○○○
21	○○○○○	51	○○○○○	81	○○○○○
22	○○○○○	52	○○○○○	82	○○○○○
23	○○○○○	53	○○○○○	83	○○○○○
24	○○○○○	54	○○○○○	84	○○○○○
25	○○○○○	55	○○○○○	85	○○○○○
26	○○○○○	56	○○○○○	86	○○○○○
27	○○○○○	57	○○○○○	87	○○○○○
28	○○○○○	58	○○○○○	88	○○○○○
29	○○○○○	59	○○○○○	89	○○○○○
30	○○○○○	60	○○○○○	90	○○○○○

A NOTE ON THE TEXT

The structure of this book is based on the Chilean Academic Aptitude Test, which students took in December each year from 1967 through 2003 in order to apply to Chilean universities. Today, students take a test with a different name (University Selection Exam) that follows a similar structure. This book specifically takes the form of the Verbal Aptitude test as it was given in 1993, the year the author took the exam. At that time it consisted of ninety multiple-choice exercises presented in five sections.